UNDERWORLDS

WHEN MONSTERS ESCAPE

TO MY FAMILY

No part of this publication may be reproduced, stored in a retrieval system, or transmitted in any form or by any means, electronic, mechanical, photocopying, recording, or otherwise, without written permission of the publisher. For information regarding permission, write to Scholastic Inc., Attention: Permissions Department, 557 Broadway, New York, NY 10012.

ISBN 978-0-545-30832-8

Text copyright © 2012 by Robert T. Abbott

Illustrations copyright © 2012 by Scholastic Inc.

All rights reserved. Published by Scholastic Inc.

SCHOLASTIC and associated logos are trademarks and/or registered trademarks of Scholastic Inc.

12 11 10 9 8 7 6 5   13 14/0

Printed in the U.S.A.   40
First printing, January 2012
DESIGNED BY TIM HALL

UNDERWORLDS

BOOK TWO

—

WHEN MONSTERS ESCAPE

BY TONY ABBOTT

ILLUSTRATED BY

ANTONIO JAVIER CAPARO

Scholastic Inc.

NEW YORK TORONTO LONDON AUCKLAND
SYDNEY MEXICO CITY NEW DELHI HONG KONG

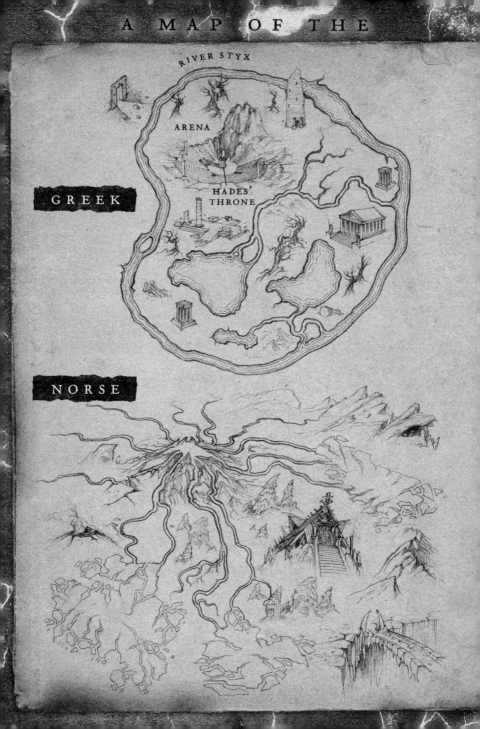

RIVER STYX

ARENA

GREEK

HADES'
THRONE

NORSE

EGYPTIAN

BABYLONIAN

CHAPTER ONE

———

A BAD DAY

My name is Owen Brown, and my forehead feels like an anvil that someone keeps pounding with a red-hot hammer.

Also my teeth hurt, my eyes sting, and my fingers ache.

But ever since my friends and I rescued Dana Runson from the Greek Underworld three days ago, pain has been the new normal—

"Owen, move it!"

Dana raced toward me across the wet school parking lot. Jon Doyle and Sydney Lamberti were right on her heels.

"Out of the way, O—" Jon yelled.

All three of them tackled me and rolled me to the side as—*whoom!*—a small car plummeted down from above, smashed onto the sidewalk, and skittered past us, sparking like fireworks, even in the rain.

Just beyond it was a giant, taller than a house, all muscles, shaggy hair . . . and one huge eye. He was a Cyclops, one of two Greek monsters who escaped from the Underworld into our town. He was ugly, he was huge, and he was mad.

Crash! An uprooted flagpole slammed down on the car and bent in half. The second giant emerged from behind the school. He was just as huge, just as mad, and just as one-eyed. But he had no hair at all.

"Run. Now!" Dana screamed, yanking me to my feet and pulling me around the side of the school, with Jon and Sydney close behind. We crouched in a puddle behind a couple of oversize trash bins, just in time to see a bike rack crumple to the ground next to the smashed car.

"What a mess from only two giants!" Sydney said, breathing hard.

"'Only two giants.' Love that," said Jon. He pulled a crooked umbrella out of the trash. The umbrella part was gone, so all that remained were the spokes. "Maybe I can use this," he said, jabbing the umbrella shaft into the air as if it were a sword.

Crash! The basketball poles from the playground bounced onto the asphalt court. Then the hairy giant started stuffing all the junk into a large sack hanging over his back.

Three days ago, Dana had been kidnapped by the Norse god Loki and trapped in the Greek Underworld. Why? We weren't exactly sure. It might have had something to do with her parents, who were in Iceland studying Norse mythology. But who knew?

Loki was one truly scary guy, with a face of smoke, and horns of frost, and a body that looked like a skeleton. Only he was alive — which he shouldn't be, as a mythological being. And he wasn't the only one. Because when Loki stashed Dana in the Greek Underworld, we had to bargain with Hades, its frightening ruler, to let her go.

The big red guy said that Dana could stay free — on one condition. Since Loki masterminded the escape of two Cyclopes from Hades' domain, Hades gave us one week to capture and return them to the Underworld. Impossible? Sure it was. Except that impossible was also the new normal.

BLAM! Another small car rolled past the trash bin and into the pile.

"What are they doing? Recycling?" I asked.

"Funny," said Jon. His eyes were wide. "Or it would be, if they weren't so big and mad."

"I'll tell you what's funny," said Sydney, looking cautiously over the top of the bin. "How did two giants escape the Underworld through our school without busting down the walls?"

Sydney was right. An entrance to the Underworld was behind the boiler room door in the basement of the school. How *did* they escape?

"And how did they stay hidden for three days?" Dana put in.

She had a point, too. We'd been on patrol for the last three days, scouring Pinewood Bluffs for the monsters. But we'd seen nothing—until tonight.

"We're not safe here," said Jon, crouching low behind the bin. "Or anywhere, really. Owen, can you put a spell on them with the lyre? Make them fall asleep or something?"

I pulled the lyre of Orpheus from the holster Sydney had made. According to what we'd read since we "borrowed" it from a museum, the lyre was made four thousand years ago by the musician Orpheus. It had seven strings and was shaped like a big horseshoe. Even though I had never played a lyre before, I found that if I plucked the right strings in the right order, I could charm people and objects to do pretty much whatever I wanted them to do.

But I wasn't sure about this time.

"The Cyclopes are so huge," I said. "They might not hear the strings correctly. Maybe I can just distract them?"

"They're turning toward downtown," Sydney said. "This could get a whole lot worse."

"Let's draw them into the woods," said Dana, glancing toward the forest behind the school. It was only suppertime, but the woods were already dark. "Owen, give the lyre a try."

"Earplugs for everyone," whispered Sydney, always practical. She pulled a plastic bag from her pocket. She, Dana, and Jon twisted the plugs into their ears as the lyre's strings jangled loudly under my fingers.

As soon as the melody blossomed into the air, time seemed to slow down for a moment. I felt dizzy. This had been happening more and more when I played the lyre. I didn't like the feeling, but the magic worked. The two giants paused in mid-mayhem and turned toward the trash bin we were hiding behind.

"Oh, I love being live bait!" Jon screeched, and we bolted to our feet. As we raced toward the forest, the wind lashed us with cold, heavy rain. The Cyclopes gathered up the wreckage in their massive sack — the bike racks, the basketball poles, even the compact cars — and stomped after us.

I kept slamming the strings as we entered the woods, and the melody coiled up through the rain like fingers, drawing the giants across the school yard. The Cyclopes were huge and lumbering, but they were charging like a couple of mad elephants.

Dana was a fast runner and she sprinted between the trees. I tried to keep up, but no sooner did I hit the woods than branches crashed behind us. Jon and Sydney scrambled quickly up a rock ledge and hurled stones at the bald Cyclops, when the ground thundered suddenly at my heels.

Dana turned. "Owen, behind you!"

The hairy Cyclops lunged at me.

Luckily, he caught his foot on a tree trunk and went down.

Unluckily, he fell right at me.

I threw myself down on the ground, cradling the lyre beneath me as the giant fell on top of me, his huge jaw inches from my face.

I couldn't bear to stare into his gross, milky eyeball. When I glanced away, I saw a round stone the size of a cheeseburger dangling from a chain around his neck. The stone was marked with strange inter-secting lines.

"De-stroy!" The Cyclops raised his great fist over my head, then suddenly bellowed, "AHHHHH!" and rolled away, clutching his giant foot — which had the point of Jon's umbrella sticking out of it.

Meanwhile, the bald giant was nursing a big bruise on his nose from where Sydney had beaned him with a rock.

"And now — we get out of here!" said Dana, pull-ing me to my feet.

We'd only made it a few steps when the giants grunted some strange words. A freezing wind sliced through the trees, nearly knocking us to the ground. Then the wind was gone. When it left and the trees settled, the two Cyclopes were gone, too.

We all stared at the empty space in front of us.

"Where did they go?" asked Dana. "How could they just . . . vanish? We can't lose track of them —"

"I wouldn't mind if they lost track of *us*," said Jon, staring all around.

"So what just happened?" asked Sydney. "Do the Cyclopes have magical powers or something?"

"No," said Dana. "Not in the usual myths, anyway."

"Monsters don't usually escape from the Underworld, either," Sydney groaned.

"Maybe this is a new myth," I said. "Either way, we have to know where they went. We need to be someplace where we can see the whole town." I stared through the trees to the coast.

Dana turned to see what I was looking at. "You don't mean . . . ?"

"I think I do."

"Are you kidding?" said Jon. "All the way up there? That's . . . dangerous!"

But my friends followed me anyway, because dangerous was also the new normal.

We dashed back across the school yard. We were going to climb the Pinewood Bluffs water tower. In a thundering rainstorm. One slippery ladder rung at a time.

CHAPTER TWO

CREW OF HEROES

THE WATER TOWER WAS A HUNDRED FEET TALL AND ringed with a narrow walkway. To get to the top, we had to climb straight up an iron ladder that was dripping with cold rainwater.

"Wherever the Cyclopes are hiding," Dana said, clinging to the rungs below me, "the tower will give us the best view."

Sydney chuckled behind her. "Also the best view of where we'll land when we fall."

"Please don't say things like that," Jon squeaked.

Poor Jon. I felt bad dragging him up there, knowing he didn't like heights. I also knew he wouldn't let us go without him.

With a final pull, I swung my arms up and around the support posts of the iron railing, crawled between them, and slumped down on the cold walkway at the top of the tower.

"The lyre's keeping dry?" asked Sydney, when she joined me.

I checked it, then pulled my hoodie tight around my head. "It's good. Dana, you have your book?"

"Safe." Dana patted the pocket of her sweatshirt.

Dana's battered copy of *Bulfinch's Mythology* had been our major source of information about the Underworlds. Besides the text, she had scribbled hundreds of notes in it. It had just about everything we needed to know about mythological places, creatures, and stories.

A lyre and a book. So far, these were our only weapons in this weird battle. Plus the sometimes-working cell phone Sydney had borrowed from her dad.

Some arsenal.

Dana squeezed up next to me. She was quiet for a few minutes, just looking out at our town. The giants were nowhere to be seen. The rain had let up a bit, but it was quickly turning into early evening, and streetlights and house lights were coming on.

"We should be home, not chasing monsters," said Dana softly.

"I told my mom we had extra work at school," I said. "Which is slightly true."

"And slightly insane," Dana added.

We all grinned at that, but Dana was serious. She had endured a lot. The unthinkable, really — being kidnapped by an evil god and held prisoner in the Underworld. I couldn't imagine it. But she wasn't wallowing. She was strong, and she was smart. Leafing through her book, she stopped at a page.

"Loki is known as the Dark Master for a reason," Dana said, referring to what the monster Argus had called Loki when we rescued her. "He was known as a trickster, too. I figure he's using tricks to get the Cyclopes to join him."

"Not to mention that gross, giant wolf, Fenrir," said Sydney.

We'd met Fenrir a couple of times, and we weren't on the best terms. He was an extra-large red-furred wolf who breathed fire and smelled like garbage.

"Actually," said Dana, "the wolf is one of Loki's children."

Jon froze. "Uh . . . what?"

Dana shook her head. "Don't ask. Loki is the father of a bunch of monsters."

"That's probably what makes him so good at getting monsters on his side. He's like a dad to them," I said, trying to make it sound funny. (Okay, so I didn't do a very good job.)

That made me think of my dad and my mom and my little sister, Mags. I hoped they would stay home and out of all this craziness.

"Dana," Sydney said, "what are the Cyclopes actually like?"

Dana brushed the rainwater from her cheeks. "They're not the sharpest crayons in the box. And they're easily enraged, which we already found out.

But they do one thing well. They make lightning bolts for Zeus."

"Do you think that's what they're doing here?" asked Sydney. "Making bolts for Loki? Was that why they were collecting metal junk?"

Dana shook her head. "I don't know."

None of us knew much, really. Only that the Underworlds were in turmoil. Loki was recruiting monsters for some big battle. But why he sent the Cyclopes here was a mystery. All I wanted was to get the giants back below and keep Dana safe.

The sky rumbled and turned blacker by the minute. Thick clouds hovered low over the buildings, the pine forests, the bluffs zigzagging the rocky shore, everything. I looked down at our small town. Nothing much was happening. The rain was keeping people inside. Good.

"It's actually kind of peaceful up here," I said.

I spoke too soon.

Out of nowhere came another fierce wind, and the two giants reappeared on the edge of the forest. They tore through the darkness outside of town, knocking down trees in their way. Then all at once, the hairy giant slowed and turned. A car was moving down the street toward the stoplight.

"Oh, no," I breathed.

The hairy Cyclops reached back and ripped a telephone pole out of the ground as if it were a weed. He threw it across the road in front of the car, which swerved up onto the sidewalk. Almost instantly, the power lines sparked, flamed, flashed brightly, and snapped, throwing the whole town — *whooom!* — into darkness. The driver leaped out of the car and ran back up the road, covering his head with a newspaper. I couldn't tell whether he saw the Cyclopes or not.

The bald giant gripped the car in one hand and dropped it into his friend's sack. Then both Cyclopes headed toward the shore.

"Where are they going?" said Jon.

We watched as the Cyclopes reached the rocks and climbed down to the water. They waded into the waves, which came up to their chests.

Then I saw it.

"They're going there," I said, pointing to a rocky island several miles up the coast. "Power Island."

The little island was a collection of dark buildings, the remains of a power plant that had been abandoned five years ago.

"It makes all the sense in the world," said Sydney slowly.

"Nothing about this makes sense!" said Jon, shaking his head. "What do the Cyclopes want out there?"

"Electricity and lightning are essentially the same thing," said Dana. "If I needed to make lightning bolts, that's where I'd go. Plus, the power plant's been empty so long, the Cyclopes can hide there without anyone seeing them."

The idea of two giants working in an old plant creeped me out.

The dark town suddenly exploded in sound. Alarms jangled. Sirens wailed. Police cars screeched up Main Avenue, their lights spinning blue and red. Fire engines lumbered out of the town's only fire station.

"Should we call our parents?" asked Jon.

"We don't want our families involved in this," I said, watching the two giants clamber up the rocky shore of the island. "We need to get over there—"

Fire-red emergency lights flashed at the school. I suddenly remembered that, because of the emergency generators and the big gym and cafeteria, the school was a community shelter during storms.

"Everyone will be going to the school," Sydney said. "What happens when we bring the giants there?"

I couldn't take my eyes off the Cyclopes dragging their sack of junk to the power plant. The idea that we would actually return them to Hades seemed so far-fetched. The fact that we had to go through the school to do it just seemed crazy and impossible.

"We'll figure that part out when we get to it," I said. "First, we follow them. Somehow."

"Our quickest way is by water," said Jon matter-of-factly. "My ship is at the docks."

Sydney turned to him. "Wait. You have a *ship*? You mean a *boat*, right? With a motor?"

"It's actually a rowboat," said Jon. "But it has oars and everything. One for each of us."

"And it's really yours?" Dana asked.

"Technically . . . no. It's my dad's," Jon said. "But it's no problem if we borrow it. When he's not looking."

It was better than nothing.

We carefully climbed down the water tower's slippery ladder to the ground and made our way quickly to the coast. When we arrived at the inlet among the bluffs, the docks were deserted. Of course they were. Nobody in his right mind would be in a boat on a night like this.

"Now . . . we take to the high seas," said Jon. We followed him to the end of the pier, where he waved his arm at the tiniest boat I'd ever seen. "Ta-da!"

"You expect us to fit into that?" Sydney said.

"Not that one," said Jon. "This one." He pointed to one even smaller.

A sudden flash of red light glowed from the distant power plant.

"The Cyclopes have already started," Dana said. "Let's move it."

The minute we climbed into the boat and rowed out beyond the rocks, the sea really let loose. Waves slapped both sides of the tiny hull at once, spraying and soaking us even more. Jon was a good sailor and knew just how to turn the boat into and against the waves, but the farther from shore we rowed, the wilder the sea became.

Sydney touched my arm. "Owen, maybe you should use the lyre to calm the sea?"

I still had no idea what power the lyre really held. Or what my dizziness meant. But we needed to get to the power plant, which sort of meant not drowning. I slipped the lyre out of its holster and hunched over it to protect it from the rain, while everyone else put in their earplugs.

As we headed into the waves, my fingers moved instinctively to the second and fifth strings. My brain seemed to swim with the sound as time rolled more slowly. I wondered how long the uncomfortable feeling would go on, but I kept playing because it was working. The waves calmed around us, and the rowboat neared the island.

The plant towering against the sky was a coal-burning facility that had shut down when a new hydroelectric power station was built a few towns over. This old place was perched on the very summit of the island. From there, a narrow flight of stairs wound down through the rocks to a short pier jutting into the sea.

"Head for that pier!" Jon yelled out. "Everyone. One. Two. Come on!"

While I played the lyre, my friends kept up the rhythm Jon set with his oar. Together we brought the boat in between the waves. Jon tucked it in under the pier and tied it to a rail.

"Jon, you're a regular Jason," I said, referring to the Greek hero who commanded a famous ship.

"Arrh!" he said, doing his best impression of Charon, the Underworld ferryman we'd met a few days before. "That'll cost you one blue penny!"

I instinctively checked my pocket. I had borrowed several pennies from Mags that morning, just in case we needed a ride from Charon later. The pennies were still there.

"Let's go," said Sydney.

Staring up the ladder, I dreaded what we'd find at the top. Fear iced my veins. But there was no time to waste. I hitched the lyre's holster on my shoulder and, one by one, we climbed the stairway up through the rocks.

CHAPTER THREE

On Power Island

By the time we reached the top of the stairs and saw the power plant up close, it was raining icy bullets. Twin smokestacks of black brick leaned over a hulk of broken windows and sunken walls. The whole place looked ghostly and dead.

Until the black windows flared with red light.

"They're definitely busy with something," Sydney said.

We took shelter under an angled coal chute and

heard sirens wailing in the distance. The town was still dark. The school was probably filling with people.

I pushed that thought out of my head. "First things first," I said. "We get inside."

"Okay," Jon said slowly. "But how did *they* get inside?"

"Right," said Dana. "How are they vanishing and reappearing? There's nothing in the myths about any magical abilities."

"Just your standard, violent one-eyed giants," said Jon. "Somehow, that doesn't cheer me up."

I suddenly remembered seeing the necklace on the hairy giant. "The giant who fell next to me had a weird stone hanging around his neck. It had marks carved all over it."

"Greek letters?" asked Sydney. "Like alpha and omega?"

I shrugged. "Maybe. I don't know Greek."

"Or was it a rune?" asked Dana. "Runes are stones that hold power, if you know the symbols and how to use them. Loki was called a Rune Master. Maybe he gave the Cyclopes magic rune stones to get them out of the Underworld. That could be how they escaped from school and vanished in the woods."

"I'm pulling up a bunch of stuff about runes now," said Sydney, tapping away on the screen of her cell. "Owen, if you can remember what the design of the rune was, we could use that same magic to get the giants back to Hades."

It seemed like a long shot, but I liked the idea of something working in our favor. "That's a better plan than mine," I said.

"I didn't know you had a plan," said Jon.

"I don't," I said. "Come on."

Carefully but quickly, we darted along the outside wall of the plant until we found a large steel door. I may not have known very much about the lyre's different powers, but I knew how to make it open doors. My friends popped in their earplugs, and I brushed the strings of the lyre until the door quivered like heat off a hot stove and popped open.

The main room of the plant was a giant open box made of coal-blackened bricks. It rose eight stories from the floor to the ceiling, where a narrow gallery was accessible only by a rickety set of stairs on the far side of the room. Part of the ceiling had crumbled in, and rain was pouring down like a waterfall, flooding a sunken section of the floor.

There was a narrow set of iron tracks around the perimeter of the room, leading deeper into the plant. The tracks had a small coal car sitting on them. Beside that, enormous machines made up of wheels and gears and pipes — generators, I guessed — seemed to have been ripped from their places and shoved to the sides of the room as if they were toys.

Against one wall was a huge coal-burning furnace. Its big iron door stood open to the room, and a fire was blazing inside. Among the flames we saw street poles, a section of bleachers, the body of a car.

"They threw all that stolen junk into the furnace," whispered Jon.

Not far away from the furnace sat a flat-topped pile of iron girders. They seemed welded together into a giant block.

"I know what that is," Sydney whispered. "Dad has one in shop class. An anvil. The Cyclopes would need a furnace *and* an anvil to make lightning bolts. This is really not good."

No, it wasn't.

But not everything was bad. Even though the room was big and open, the piles of equipment pushed aside to make room for the anvil created tunnels and shadows where we could hide if we needed to.

And we needed to — fast.

Something heavy scraped across the floor deep inside the plant, and we took cover behind a mess of busted machines.

Scrape. Pause. *Scrape.* And something the size of a mountain moved into the room.

In the light from the blazing furnace, we saw one of the giants clearly for the first time.

If he was huge when we saw him outside school, he seemed to have grown. To call him a giant hardly seemed big enough. The guy was gargantuan. He was almost as tall as the eight-story room itself. He lumbered in slowly, every muscle in his massive arms and legs clenched and menacing.

His head was the size of a hot-air balloon. Shaggy

hair hung in tangled clumps to his shoulders, which were as wide as a house. Under a brow as big as a hedge stood one large, round, wet eye.

"Gross . . ." Jon said, swallowing behind his hand. "I think I'm going to—"

I knew how he felt.

The white of the monster's one huge eye was the color of eggnog. The brown pupil at the center pulsed, causing the eye to drool yellow liquid down his cheeks.

A wave of nausea moved from my stomach up to my throat. I breathed deep and swallowed hard.

From his massive shoulders to his knees, the Cyclops wore a kind of blacksmith's apron that looked patched together from a whole herd of cattle.

Dana crept up beside me, nudging me to look at the giant's massive hand. In it, he held a hammer with a head the size of a garbage can.

The floor thundered and now the hairless giant entered, casting his big eye on the anvil. "The Dark Master freed us for one thing only," he bellowed in a voice like rolling thunder. "He needs it fast."

The hairy giant nodded. "The forge is hot. Let us begin," he said in the same way.

"They're each wearing one of those necklaces," I whispered, creeping as close as I dared.

Together, the two giants took a big pair of tongs, dragged something out of the furnace, and dropped it on the anvil.

FWA-A-A-ANG!

A blinding crash of light flared from the anvil, blasting the room with heat. The giants laughed, then positioned themselves on either side of the anvil. Raising their hammers, they began to pound the hot metal. *Doom! Doom! Doom!* First one Cyclops hammered, then the other, over and over, until the metal on the anvil began to take shape.

Putting down his hammer, the hairy giant reached for the tongs and tossed the hammered object into the huge pool of rainwater. *SSSSS!* The water exploded with steam, filling the room with a nasty-smelling cloud. Both Cyclopes coughed and tried to wave the steam away.

As the bald giant thundered over another piece of

metal at the anvil, the hairy one dragged the cooled piece out of the pool and drew a long file from his apron. With each stroke, the metal lost its crude shape. He ran the file over and over the metal, until it was as bright as silver and shone with brilliant light.

Dana groaned softly. "And that's how they make lightning bolts."

Piece after piece went from the forge to the anvil to the cooling pool. After Baldy hammered them, Hairy polished them, making the pieces so bright they were almost impossible to look at. Shielding my eyes, I glimpsed one piece shaped like a silver platter the size of a breakfast table. Another was a long tube bent at a right angle. One of the others looked like a large hand with blades running along the fingers.

Jon tapped my shoulder. "I haven't seen a lot of actual lightning bolts up close," he whispered, "but none of that stuff looks like lightning."

The bald Cyclops removed one last piece from the pool and held it up. It was a large cone, made of bands of metal crisscrossing one another and twisting to a point at the top.

I didn't know what it was, but I knew what it looked like.

A helmet.

"Uh-oh." Dana's face was suddenly as pale and frightened as when she had disappeared to the Underworld. "They're not making lightning bolts for Loki. They're making armor!"

"Yes, yes!" Sydney whispered, tapping on her cell. "I just saw something about Loki's armor. According to legend, Loki was wounded by Odin, the chief Norse god. He was hurt so severely, he couldn't be healed."

Dana nodded quickly. "My parents told me that. He was seriously hurt, but he couldn't die. Though armor made by the Cyclopes would be . . . indestructible . . ."

My brain sparked with a crazy idea. "If this armor is for Loki," I whispered, "and we trapped the Cyclopes *and* wrecked the armor, it would solve two problems."

"Hold on, look at this," whispered Sydney, pushing her phone in front of us. "It's an alphabet of rune symbols. Owen, did you see any of these runes on the necklace?"

LOKI'S HELMET

I studied the strange carvings and pointed to one of them. "There were a couple on the stone. That was the biggest one."

"Thurisaz," Dana whispered. "Of course. Owen, I should have remembered that when you first told us about the necklace. Thurisaz is Loki's special rune. He uses it to control shape-shifting. The Cyclopes must have used it to get out of the Underworld, out of our school, and to vanish in the woods."

"Then we'll use it on the giants to capture them," Sydney said.

"Okay," whispered Jon. "But how will we get that close to them?"

Before anyone could answer, the hairy Cyclops stood and stretched his mighty arms. "Done?"

"Done." The bald giant clanged his hammer suddenly on the empty anvil.

And all at once, a passage in the far corner of the big room thundered with the sound of marching feet.

Hundreds and hundreds of feet.

CHAPTER FOUR

DEATH WALKERS

"SOMEONE'S COMING!" I WHISPERED. "LOTS OF SOME-ones!"

Syd covered her nose and mouth. "Oh! The smell—"

The huge room filled with the stench of decay as an army of creatures entered the plant. I almost choked. They were large, bearded men, their eyes hollow and black. Their pale skin—what there was of it—was sagging off of steely white bones. Animal skins draped their shoulders, and bits and pieces of rusty gray armor covered their chests.

They stomped and scraped and dragged themselves in, printing the floor with what looked like melting snow. There must have been a hundred of them.

As if they weren't scary enough, they carried big broadswords of rusty iron.

"They're . . . dead!" whispered Jon.

"Draugs," Dana muttered, her fingers flipping the pages of her book. "My parents told me legends about them. I never believed they really existed."

"Who—or *what*—are Draugs?" asked Sydney.

"Draugs are 'death walkers,'" Dana said. "Dead Viking warriors who come back, like ghosts. After they die, their souls live on in their old dead form. Draugs are strong. Angry. Evil. And they can't really die."

"Perfect," Jon groaned.

"Look, another rune," I said, squinting at the Draugs. "The head dead guy has one. They're all under Loki's power."

Behind the Draugs were several dead horses, also armored. The horses stopped at the pile of armor cooling on the floor. They pawed at the stones with their black hooves.

"They're here for the armor," said Sydney. "But where are they going to take it?"

I almost didn't want to know.

The Draugs didn't speak a word to the Cyclopes, who merely stepped back to watch the dead men fill the coal car with silver armor. The Vikings then hitched the horses to the coal car. One Draug uttered a sharp word, and with a terrible shriek, the horses moved and the car began to roll along the tracks toward the passage.

"Do you think the dead guys are taking the armor to Loki right now?" whispered Jon. "Is he that close to us? Oh, man. This is bad."

As we stood in the shadows, hiding from the Cyclopes and watching a bunch of dead Vikings take indestructible armor to an evil creep, my brain started whirring. It was telling me I was a coward if I didn't do something. This was the same part of my brain that got me involved in every club and cause at school. It's what made me go after Dana when she was in the Underworld.

I turned to my friends. "Look, guys, we can't walk away from this. We can't *not* do something."

Jon narrowed his eyes at me. "What are you saying?"

"Exactly what you think I'm saying," I said. "If we really are in the middle of a war, and it's in our world, and we have a chance to do something about it, we have to try. No one else is here. It's only us."

"But we have to capture the Cyclopes for Dana to stay with us," said Sydney, glancing at Dana. "We might miss our chance if we follow these stinky dead people."

"We can do both," said Dana, "with the runes."

Jon turned to her. "Now what are *you* saying?"

"If we can steal the runes from the giants," Dana said, "maybe we can find a way to shape-shift and follow the Draugs. The Cyclopes can't get out of the power plant without the runes, so we don't have to worry about that. Between Sydney's cell phone and my notes, we can probably find a way to make the runes work for us."

Jon shook his head. As I watched the Draugs march out of the room, I wasn't sure, either. Dana's idea seemed awfully risky.

"The giants may be a little light in the brain department," I said, "but look at them. How can we steal something from around their necks? They're huge. We're just a bunch of nobodies."

Sydney drew in a short breath. "Great idea, Owen." She tapped her forehead. "It's all in Dana's book. The famous story of Odysseus escaping the Cyclopes by blinding them and saying that Nobody did it."

Jon winced. "Blinding them?"

"Odysseus did it for real," Sydney said. "But we can do it with smoke. We push them back near that walkway, snatch the runes from around their necks, and follow the Draugs. But to make it all happen, Owen, we need a little musical accompaniment. . . ."

After she explained it, I had to admit that Sydney's idea was a good one.

Step One: Use the lyre to force smoke into the

Cyclopes' eyes. Step Two: With the smoke as a shield, climb the stairs to the walkway near the ceiling. Step Three: Snatch the runes from around the necks of the giants (keeping them trapped in the power plant). Step Four: Use the runes to make us look like Draugs.

Okay, maybe those last two steps were as hazy as the smoke, but we didn't have time to overthink it. "Time for earplugs," I whispered. "Here goes nothing—"

I plucked the lyre, tentatively at first, feeling that familiar rush of dizziness. Then I found the notes I needed.

I played them over and over until— *whoosh!* —thick smoke collected inside the forge and poured out the open door into the room. Slowing and then speeding up the melody, I made the smoke rise directly into the giants' faces.

"Hey!" growled Baldy, as black haze billowed up at him like smoke from a barbeque.

The hairy Cyclops grunted. "What's happening?"

Both of them began coughing and wheezing. Trying

desperately to get out of the smoke, they backed away from the furnace and moved toward the walkway.

Sydney grinned. "Perfect. Now for Step Two."

While she and Dana searched the cell phone and the book for details about rune magic, Jon and I scrambled up the stairs as quickly as we could. I kept playing the lyre as I climbed, which wasn't easy since my head was spinning and the old steps squealed and wobbled all the way up.

"Who's there?" boomed the bald giant from inside the cloud of smoke.

"Nobody! I'm over here!" Dana yelled, drawing the giants back toward the walkway.

"Hah!" shouted the hairy Cyclops, grabbing at the air. "We'll get you, Nobody!"

Jon and I made it to the top of the stairs and ran around the walkway as the two giants staggered back toward us. They—and their rune necklaces—were only a few feet away.

"Come on," I whispered. "Come on. One more step . . ."

I still didn't have a clear idea of how we would get

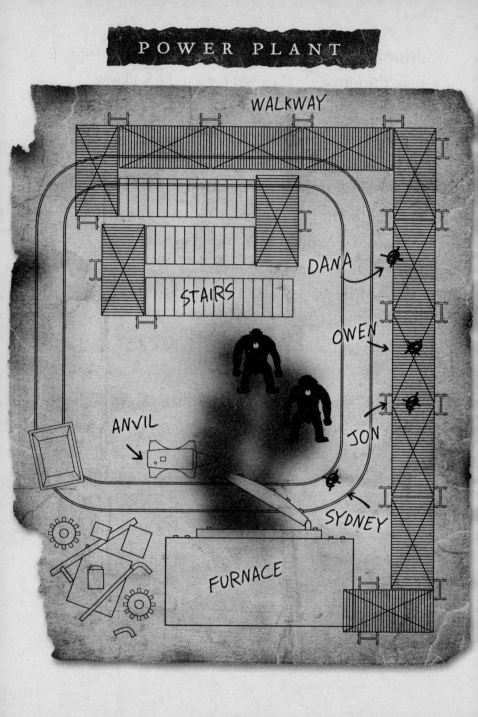

the runes from around the giants' monster-size necks, but I didn't have to.

"Cover me," said Jon.

"Cover you?" I repeated.

Before I could stop him, Jon climbed over the walkway railing, leaped three feet across open air, and latched on to the hairy Cyclops's neck.

The hairy giant lurched and grabbed at his throat frantically, trying to remove Jon's hands. The bald Cyclops couldn't see, but flailed away with his fists, striking the wall next to me. I dodged the bricks falling onto the walkway. Jon clung to the rune necklace and screamed at the top of his lungs. Sydney and Dana dived away from the crashing bricks. I nearly fell to my death.

Then it really got crazy.

CHAPTER FIVE

INTO THE EYE OF THE STORM

WHILE I HELD ON TO THE SHAKY WALKWAY, THE shaggy giant clawed at his neck like he couldn't breathe. Jon clung to the rune as if it was a life preserver. The bald Cyclops stumbled away from the walkway, his face still wrapped in smoke. Dana hurled bricks at his knees while Sydney shoveled hot coals onto his feet.

"Ahhh! No! I'll get you!" he boomed.

"The name is Nobody!" Syd yelled back. "Don't forget it!"

"Owen —" Jon screamed as he spun around and around the giant's fat neck.

I slammed the lyre with my palm, and the hairy Cyclops bellowed in pain, arching back into the wall next to me. I grabbed the necklace with both hands and pulled.

SNAP! The necklace broke, sending sparks of electricity everywhere, and Jon fell back into me. The hairy giant howled, "My stone! Nobody stole my stone!" He wheeled angrily toward the walkway.

Jon jumped to his feet. "What about the other rune? Don't we need both?"

The bald Cyclops shielded his neck and backed away.

"We'll have to make it work with one," I said. "Now . . . run!"

Flang! Flang! I tweaked out a solo as Jon and I raced down the squeaky stairs. "I hear Nobody!" the hairy giant yelled. "Stop, Nobody!"

But we were on the ground, running as fast as our legs could carry us.

"Into the passage," said Dana. She sprinted into the darkness like an Olympic runner. After all, she had the most to lose if we failed. We rushed after her into a passage that was strangely cold. The floor was slippery, almost icy.

"This is weird," said Dana, sliding to a stop. "Why is it so icy? It's almost like . . ." She paused. "The Draugs came in with snowy boots. Did anyone see that?"

"I did," I said.

"What about it?" Sydney asked.

Dana shook her head. "I don't know yet. We'd better keep going or we'll lose the Draugs."

"This stone tingles," said Jon, hurrying behind me with the rune stone at arm's length. "And not in a good way. It feels weird."

I thought about the odd sensation I felt when I played the lyre. Maybe that was the thing about magic—you paid a price for using it.

Sydney edged forward in the icy passage and

stopped at a turn. "There they are," she whispered. We joined her in time to see the distant caravan of dead men, horses, and silver armor up ahead. "Just before my cell lost its signal, I found something out," she said. "It's not good. Everything I've seen about runic shape-changing magic says that you need a piece of the thing you want to change into."

"You mean something from a Draug?" said Dana, eyeing the forms ahead of us.

We all looked at one another, then at the disgusting dead men, then at one another again. No one moved.

"Seriously?" I muttered. "I can't believe I'm doing this."

Without thinking a whole lot, I sped quietly down the icy passage. I crept up behind the last dead Viking. The stench was almost overpowering. Holding my breath, I reached out . . . and the Draug stopped and turned.

I flattened myself to the freezing cold ground just in time. The Viking swiveled his head back up the passage and peered into the gloom. That was my chance. I plucked a single thread from a rag dangling from his rotten boot. After what seemed like an eternity, the Draug turned back and caught up with the other dead guys. I stayed motionless on the ground for a minute before I slunk back to my friends. "Something like this?" I said, holding up the thread and finally letting out my breath.

"Exactly like that," said Sydney. Then she grinned. "By the way, you're elected to do all the gross stuff from now on."

I didn't laugh. I also didn't like the idea of transforming into a Draug. But there wasn't time to think it through. Between Syd's dying cell phone and Dana's scribbled notes, we came up with a few words that might make it happen. We all grabbed hold of the Draug thread and chanted strange runic names over and over. The rune stone turned from stony gray to silver.

And our appearance began to change.

We grew larger, wider, our faces oozed facial hair — even the girls' — and our clothes turned gray and frayed. In moments, we resembled the dead Viking warriors, all bones and rotten skin, from our dented helmets to our rag-booted feet. We didn't feel dead. We just looked like it.

"How do I look?" asked Jon.

"Pretty dead to me," I said. "How about me?"

"If you weren't my best friend, I'd be scared," he said.

Dana gave a wry grin. "Then let's mingle with the dead guys."

We moved as fast as we could to the end of the passage, and into the next one and the next, frantically trying to come up with a plan. The best we could do was based on something Dana found in her notes. Loki's armor might be indestructible only if all of it was there. So we just had to snatch a piece of the armor and take off before anyone noticed. Somehow.

How hard could that be?

I knew we would find out really soon.

My brain was screaming in my skull by the time we got to the end of the Draug force. Holding our breaths, we tried, slowly and casually, to make our way up through the ranks toward the coal car. But

THE DRAUGS

we couldn't get close enough. The troop of dead men crowded around the car, so we had to keep marching deeper and farther into the passages.

I can't say how long we were trudging along, but it must have been miles. Finally the passage opened up, and we were suddenly outside, on a vast stretch of snow and ice.

I didn't like it. Home seemed a thousand miles away. Maybe it was.

"Where *are* we?" Sydney whispered.

In the distance was a range of snow-streaked black mountains. Behind them I could see the flattened cone of a gigantic volcano.

"I don't know," Dana said softly, narrowing her eyes. "But it doesn't look Greek. It looks very . . . Norse."

My heart stuck in my throat. No way. No. A *second* Underworld?

A giant snowstorm whirled in the distance. The spinning snow roared like a jet engine, but as if it were nothing, the Draugs walked straight into the storm. So did the horses drawing the coal car.

And so did we.

The air was black and rushing inside the storm, but we didn't blow away, and it didn't last long. Beyond the spinning snow was a clearing in a stand of tall trees. It was shadowed and cold, but calm. The eye of the snowstorm.

In front of us stood a cluster of tree trunks that came to a point overhead. It was pitch-black beneath the arch, almost like we were looking into a cave. At its mouth stood a cauldron, boiling with dark blue liquid.

This wasn't good.

The horses and Draugs stopped in the clearing. A moment or two later, a voice came from the darkness under the arch of trees.

The dead horses stopped pawing the icy ground.

Everything hushed.

"Have the giants-s-s done my bidding?" the voice hissed.

The Draugs next to us bowed. We did, too.

"And the armor is-s-s ready?"

It was Loki's voice, no doubt about it.

"Then bring it," Loki said. "Bring it to me . . . now!"

CHAPTER SIX

Out of Thick Air

Like firefighters handing water buckets down a line, a bunch of dead Vikings unloaded armor from the coal car and passed it along to the others, including Jon, Dana, Sydney, and me.

I was tempted to steal a chunk of armor and bolt back through the storm. I'm sure we all were. But the dead eyes of the Draugs were everywhere and we were way outnumbered. If I could read my friends' minds, I was sure they'd all say the same thing: "Remind me again why we're doing this?" But we'd have to wait for another chance.

Soon the coal car was empty. We stacked Loki's heavy silver armor into a pile by the mouth of the cave. I could hear the sound of breath from within the darkness.

When Loki stepped out of the shadows, I saw him up close for the first time. My insides twisted. The only other time I had seen him, at the tower when we rescued Dana, was no more than a glimpse. He'd ridden on the back of Fenrir, his enormous red wolf. He'd been moving. There was smoke. We were afraid. We didn't get a good look.

But now, so close that I wanted to be anywhere else, I saw that Loki really had been horribly wounded.

As he came toward us, he dragged his right leg behind him. His left arm hung limp at his side. Dangling lifelessly from it was a white, skeletal hand. The cloak over his shoulders hid a powerful frame that was bent and weakened.

Worst of all was his face.

It seemed like it was made of smoke—moving, changing, and dark, with a sense of evil about it. On top of his head were horns of twisted ice. And there was a scar. It traveled like a deep trench from his right eyebrow across his nose and cheek to his lips. The scar was what caused him to hiss.

Then Loki spoke at the cauldron in a raspy voice. "Come forth, my northern friend!" At once, the blue liquid spat more fiercely. A form grew out of the steam rising from the cauldron—the face of a woman. She was hideous, blue-skinned, with black lips, dark holes for eyes, and hair like a mass of writhing blue snakes. I felt Jon quiver beside me. I nudged him as if to say, *Yeah, I'm terrified, too.*

"You move quickly," the woman said to Loki. Her voice sounded like an echo returning from far away.

Loki turned back to the shadows and hissed a brief command. Fenrir appeared from the blackness, wearing a spiked collar. A pair of reins ran from the collar to a long sledge on rails, made of oak timbers. As Fenrir dragged the sledge over the ice, we saw that its planks were carved with strange symbols.

Runes. I glanced over at Sydney and Dana. They had noticed them, too.

Loki smiled. "I control many things with my magical stones. They are how I managed the Cyclopes' es-s-scape. They are how I race from world to world."

"Why do you call the ancient oracle from her sleep?" the woman said.

"To s-s-secure the future of my plans," Loki hissed, his eyes flashing. "Watch closely."

Loki pulled a large piece of silver armor from the pile—a breastplate. It was three feet wide at least. Loki swung his cloak back to attach the massive thing, and I swear I caught a glimpse of rib bone where his chest should be. I tried not to lose my lunch. Then he took another piece and strapped it onto his wounded leg.

As we watched silently, Loki became an armored man.

"Impressive," said the blue-faced oracle.

Loki's scarred lips pursed into a cold smile. "My war begins. The world above will be the battlefield.

Now that I am armed, I can proceed. But tell me of the Crystal Rune. . . ."

"The key to Asgard?" the woman said.

I tried not to show my surprise. Asgard. The home of the Norse gods. The court of Odin.

"The two humans are close on the rune's trail in Iceland," she said.

Dana let out a quiet gasp. "Nooooo . . ."

I brushed against her shoulder. I knew. The two humans the oracle mentioned might be Dana's parents. That couldn't be good.

"One day more and they will have that which you seek," the woman intoned.

Great. What was that supposed to mean? Couldn't these people speak normally?

Loki scoffed. "Then this very hour, I shall release my . . . *creatures*. They shall s-s-stop the meddlers. The Crystal Rune will be mine."

I shall release my creatures. Stop the meddlers. If he was talking about Dana's parents, I couldn't imagine what was going through her mind right then.

Raising his one good hand, Loki turned to Fenrir. The wolf leaned to its master, its yellow fangs dripping liquid that hissed on the icy ground between its front paws. I couldn't hear what Loki said, but then he raised his head and turned to the oracle.

"I take a journey soon," he said. "But in two days' time, I will have everything I need."

The oracle smiled. "There are others against you. The three children and the girl they rescued. I sense them close to you now."

I shivered from head to toe.

"No human in history has visited more than one of the Underworlds," Loki said.

The words struck me. We had rescued Dana from the Greek Underworld. Were we in the Norse one now? Had we done something no one had done before?

All at once, Loki swung his head around to us. I almost screamed.

"You, Draugs!" he snapped. "You shall remain behind. Destroy the children. Capture the girl. I can use her. But destroy the other three!"

It felt really wrong to bow in agreement, but we had to.

Loki turned again to the oracle. "Before I dis-miss-s-s you and s-s-secure the final piece of my puzzle, conjure me a vision of the days-s-s to come——"

Smoke blossomed around the face of the blue woman. Hideous creatures took shape in the haze. Monsters——spiked, clawed, fire-breathing——crawled and slithered and flew across miles of golden sand, destroying everything they touched.

That scene merged into the next, where those same monsters raced through our world. I saw towns, villages, cities turned to ashes. The water tower in Pinewood Bluffs toppled in flames. The buildings on Main Avenue, including our school, were piles of smoking rubble. My knees felt weak. It was horrible. But I couldn't look away.

This scene melted into another, showing the same creatures attacking a giant wooden hall nestled in mountains of ice and snow.

I guessed it was Asgard, the home of the Norse gods. Odin's house.

So, first the Underworlds. Then our world. Then the throne of Odin.

Loki would attack them all.

When the vision finally faded, Loki took one of the last pieces of armor from the dwindling pile — the helmet. He slid it over his head. It clicked into place. It was magnificent and horrible at the same time, a helmet of silver bands that wove around and between the icy horns on his head.

"I venture now to a far land," he said. "When I return, no one shall keep me from sitting on Odin's throne." His voice was clear and deep. He no longer hissed his words.

We watched Loki produce a stone from inside his cloak. It was carved with shape-shifting runes. He fitted it into a notch on his breastplate, then picked up the last piece of armor. It was the left-hand glove I had seen being forged, the one for his lifeless hand. It shimmered in the firelight.

"With this final fragment of armor," he said, "I become whole once more."

Dana leaned close to my ear. "He'll be unstoppable. We have to do something—"

Suddenly, the snowstorm parted and the bald Cyclops stumbled among us, half his giant size, rubbing his eyes and groaning with each step.

"They—escaped!" he exclaimed.

"Who escaped?" Loki demanded.

I could see the giant thinking hard. Then he brightened. "Nobody! I remember. Nobody escaped!"

"Fool!" Loki shouted at the giant. "Don't you read your own myths?" He whipped his one gloved hand at the Cyclops, and a bolt of light blasted out.

Just then, the blue woman shot up from the smoke and thrust a blue finger at the four of us. "The children!" she screamed, vanishing into the freezing air.

All at once our disguises fell to the ice. The filthy shrouds bunched around our ankles, and we were suddenly ourselves again.

"Uh-oh," Jon said.

"Time to run!" yelled Sydney.

Which I thought was a really good idea, but Dana broke away from the rest of us. "We're not leaving empty-handed!" She leaped over to Loki. "You creep! Leave my parents alone —"

And before Loki could react, she slammed into him, which didn't budge him an inch. He flung her away with a flick of his wrist, but when Dana fell to the ground, she was holding a single silver glove as if it were a hot potato.

"*Now* we get out of here!" she cried, and leaped right past the startled dead men.

CHAPTER SEVEN

WHEN KIDS ESCAPE

"DRAUGS!" CRIED LOKI. "TAKE HER. DESTROY THE others!"

As the ghost warriors hurled themselves at us, I whipped out the lyre and thumbed the lowest string. *Thoommmm!* Time slowed for an instant, but it was all the distraction we needed.

"Hold hands!" I shouted. The four of us plunged into the whirling wall of snow.

Furious, Loki burst through the storm, sending

fire bolts slicing across the air and exploding at our heads. At the same time, he touched the rune on his breastplate. The entire suit of armor began to move, growing into his body and turning him silver from head to toe.

"Whoa . . ." I breathed.

The helmet wove bands of silver over his face. The horns on his head stuck out of the helmet and writhed as if alive. His smoky face was half visible through the crisscrossing bands—and so was his deep, long scar.

Over it all, we could hear Loki scream out his runic magic.

Dana's face was tight with pain and fear. Clutching her with one hand and Sydney (who held on to Jon) with the other, I plowed deep into the icy passages that led back to the power plant. We hurried through the tunnels, barely staying ahead of Loki and the Draugs.

We were escaping . . . until Dana fell behind.

"Dana, what is it?" I said.

She suddenly crumpled to the passage floor and cried out, "My hand!"

I bent to help her up, then stopped. Loki's armored glove was *forming around* her hand. It melted over her wrist and palm and fingers like liquid silver.

"It burns so much!" she said.

"Get it off of her!" Sydney cried. But as soon as she grasped Dana's arm, she jerked her fingers back. "It's freezing!"

Dana sucked in a breath. Her eyes rolled up into her head. We heard the clatter of the Draugs and dead horses behind us.

"Dana," I whispered, "we need to—"

"I know!" she snapped, jumping to her feet. The silver still moved over her fingers, growing from her elbow to her fingertips like molten silver.

"That glove is alive," said Jon in awe. "Like the rest of Loki's armor."

The thunder of horses' hooves rang through the passage.

"Dana, don't worry," I said, urging her forward. "We'll get it off. The lyre can—"

"No!" she said, gritting her teeth. "Not yet. Without

this hand, he's not complete. This glove might help us—"

All at once, a bolt of razor-sharp light exploded from Dana's silver fingertips. We were thrown against the icy walls of the passage. The shot hit the ceiling overhead, raining chunks of ice down on us. Another bolt shot wildly behind us. The Draug horses reared and the dead men scattered.

"Whoa!" Jon cried. "Lethal weapon!"

The bald Cyclops was in the tunnel now, bounding toward us, his shoulders scraping the jagged icy walls. The rune was keeping him smaller than normal, but he still barreled easily through the Draugs.

"Come on," said Dana, pushing us toward the power plant with her normal hand.

"Dana," I said, "are you sure—"

"I'm fine," she said, her eyes still wide. "And now we have our weapon!"

A trio of Draugs clambered up the passage and leaped at us before we could get to the end. Jon ducked out of the way. Dana spun like a ballerina, and blades of light swung around her like scythes.

The ragged shrouds of the Draugs caught fire.

"Man, she is good!" said Jon, running ahead again.

"And on our side!" Sydney added.

Another group of Draugs pushed its way through, hacking wildly with their axes and spears, but Dana deflected them all.

"Brother!" called the bald Cyclops as we approached the entrance to the plant. I realized that the other one, still a giant, was probably waiting for us — and was probably mad. But we had nowhere else to go. We raced into the big, open room.

"Take cover," Dana said, dragging us all behind a crumpled generator.

She swung her heavy silver hand toward the furnace. A single, narrow bolt flashed from her fingertips, and the furnace exploded.

The attacking Draugs catapulted head over heels into the giants, who swatted them away like flies. I slammed backward into the brick wall. Bricks crashed around me. More flashes of light shot from Dana's hand, and more bricks fell like rain. I don't know if I passed out or what, but when the smoke cleared, the Draugs and their dead horses were nowhere to be seen.

"Did we win?" asked Jon.

"Not yet," said Sydney. "We still need to trap the Cyclopes!"

Both giants were full size now. They were mad—and getting madder. They started banging on the walls with their enormous hammers, hoping to crush us under a rain of bricks. A crack appeared in the wall behind the forge. It quickly spread up the side to the ceiling. Bricks cascaded to the floor as the wall separated. The entire room was crumbling, while fire spilled from the furnace onto the floor.

"We need to get out of here!" I shouted.

"Not yet!" said Dana. She aimed her silver hand at the forge. A lightning bolt blew out of the forge and struck the wall above Baldy's head. I didn't know how Dana was learning to use the glove so fast—but I was glad she was.

Ka-boom! Bricks tumbled on both Cyclopes.

Dana kept throwing bolts of silvery light at the bricks until the entire wall crumbled. With a tremendous *thud*, the giants fell backward onto the ground outside the plant.

"Loki could return any second," said Jon, rain pouring down his face.

"Not this way, he won't!" said Dana. She destroyed the passage entrance with one final blast. Then we staggered away from the plant.

"Back, giants! Get — back!" Dana was unstoppable. With her hand streaming fiery light, she forced the giants to the edge of the rocks. The sea howled behind them.

"We're taking you back!" I called to them. "To Hades' Underworld!"

Dana twisted her gloved hand in the air. I knew it hurt her. I could tell by the pain on her face and in her eyes. But Loki's glove had magic. Thick chains swirled suddenly out of the storm like snakes and wound around the Cyclopes' wrists, binding the giants tightly together.

We had captured them.

"Woo-hoo!" Jon cheered.

Behind us, the power plant was an inferno.

"We can't stay here," I said. "We need to get back to the school, fast. Any ideas?"

Jon grinned. "Let's make the giants tow us back to shore. Captain Jason, at your service!"

"Perfect," said Dana, nodding firmly.

Threatened by her sparking fist, the two Cyclopes stepped into the water. We chained them to the front of Jon's rowboat. I pulled out the lyre and turned to Dana. "The lyre of Orpheus and the magic armor of Loki. Is there anything in your book like this?"

Dana shook her head. "Nope. We're writing our own mythology now."

That seemed just right to me.

"Earplugs!" I shouted.

My fingers found the right notes on the lyre. First string. Second string. Sixth string. Fifth string. The waves calmed.

Looking odder than just about anything I could imagine, the towering one-eyed giants from Greek mythology tugged our tiny boat back to shore.

CHAPTER EIGHT

THE LYRE AND
THE GLOVE

"FASTER!" JON SHOUTED UP AT THE CYCLOPES.

The giants lumbered powerfully through the waves, bound tightly in chains, tugging our boat behind them. I kept plucking the strings of the lyre, and the water stayed as peaceful as in a baby's bathtub.

"At least we trapped the Cyclopes," Jon said. "That should make Hades happy."

"I doubt Hades is ever happy," said Sydney. "And

he'll be even *not* happier when he hears about Loki's plans."

That was true, but in that moment I felt like we had done something pretty incredible. We'd found and captured two enormous giants. Us! I mean, yeah, we had the help of a magical lyre, and some kind of superglove. But still. This was a real victory.

I also knew that this might be nothing compared to what lay ahead for our world, if Loki fulfilled his plans. Was he really going to use our world as a stepping-stone between the Underworlds and the house of the gods? And there was the other thing. Loki was sending his creatures to stop Dana's parents from finding the Crystal Rune, the key to Asgard.

I turned to Dana. Her face was so pale. "You know that keeping you free is the most important thing right now," I said.

She looked at me, questioning. "I keep thinking . . . my parents . . ."

"After you're safe, we'll find a way to stop Loki from . . . whatever he's doing," I said firmly.

"It will be dangerous," she said.

"I know," I said. "We all know. Sydney, have you figured out how to use the rune to shrink these guys yet?"

"Working on it," she said, tapping on her cell phone.

"The electricity is still out," said Jon, pointing to the darkness in Pinewood Bluffs. "Which should help us get the Cyclopes through the streets."

"It's getting colder," Dana said, shivering.

I couldn't feel it at first, because I was already so cold, but Dana was right. The rain had begun to freeze into little pellets. We'd already been through one snowstorm. If felt like we were heading into another.

Thanks to the giants' big strides, it wasn't long before we were back at the docks.

"Halt!" Jon called out. He was taking his job as captain very seriously. And as he predicted, the blackout across town turned out to be a great cover for us. We moved up the rocks, onto the bluffs, and along the empty back streets.

We almost made it the whole way, too.

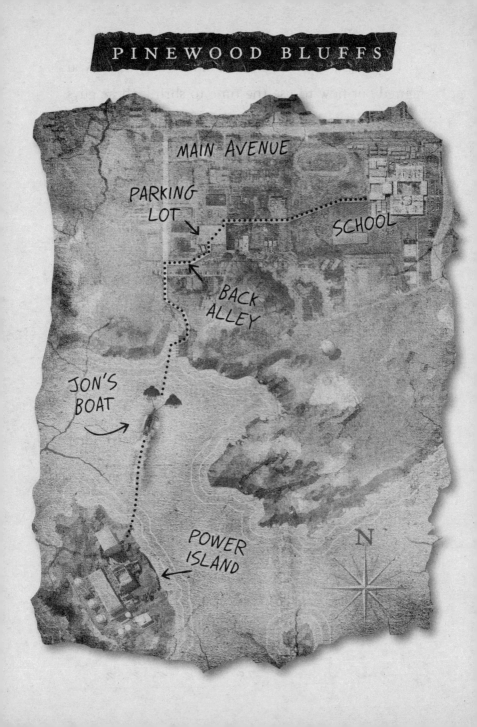

Then, only minutes from the school, we heard the undeniable stomping of dead feet.

"Them again?" said Jon.

Them again. A dozen ghostly Draugs, four of them mounted, stomped out from behind a corner and stood in our way. Their axes were poised and ready for battle.

"How did they get here?" asked Sydney.

"They must have made it out of the plant somehow," said Dana. "Or there's another exit from the Underworld."

"Which nobody wants to think about right now," said Jon, groaning. "Anyone for running and hiding?"

Just then, the Draugs advanced.

"Quick, this way!" said Dana. "And that means you Cyclopes, too!"

We dragged the growling Cyclopes with us down an alley next to the movie theater. The Draugs chased us, heaving their axes. The blades clanked on the asphalt. We rushed to the other end of the street, next to the bank. From there, it was an open parking lot all the way to the grocery store.

"It's too far to run in the open," Jon said, looking around.

"We fight," said Dana, giving me a grim face.

I sighed. "This is turning into a very long day. Earplugs!"

I blasted a solo on the lyre — the same one I'd used to put Argus to sleep. It didn't have the same effect on the ghostly Draugs, but it did slow their advance. This gave Dana time to whip her gloved hand in a circle. A spiral of light shot through the air like an angry whip and caught one Viking on the neck. He flew off his feet with a scream and tumbled into the Draugs behind him. While Jon and Sydney hustled the giants behind the bank, Dana and I took on the group of dead men like a couple of real heroes.

We held the sluggish Draugs off for a while, too, but they kept picking themselves back up. Even with Dana's glove blasting everywhere, the Draugs pushed us across the parking lot, finally trapping us between the front of the store and a delivery truck.

That's when I heard the sound of thumping in the air behind us.

The Valkyries.

Three enormous winged horses emerged from the clouds. On their backs, in sparkling armor, sat three spear-toting warriors.

"Hoyo-toho!" the riders cried in unison as their massive horses swooped down like lightning. The one called Doom Rider, otherwise known as Miss Hilda, the head lunch lady, jerked her spear into the midst of the Draugs. "You shall go *back* where you came from!" she cried. Then she uttered some words to the dead Vikings, who seemed to understand her. (Which made sense, since they were from the same myth.) But when Soul Snatcher—Miss Marge—charged her steed directly into the ghosts, the dead guys broke ranks and fled into the streets.

"Sisters!" cried Miss Lillian—otherwise known as Death Maiden. "Attack without mercy!"

A barrage of icicles shot from the tips of the ladies' spears like the blast of machine guns. *B-b-b-b-b-bam!* Windows shattered all along Main Avenue. Jon and Sydney cried out as the Cyclopes tried to break free, but Dana ran back to secure them.

Eventually, the Valkyries were too fast for the troop of dead men. They swooped on the Draugs and ran them down, every one — horses, too — snaring them in an iron net the size of my house. Then they dragged them across the parking lot to the grocery store.

"We will return these outlaws to face judgment in Odin's court," Soul Snatcher said through her frightening winged helmet.

"There are dire events in all of the Underworlds, and Loki is the cause," said Miss Hilda.

"He has released dragons from the Norse Underworld of Niflheim. The dragons have mercilessly destroyed a village in your world," added Death Maiden, staring fiery-eyed.

"Loki said he was releasing creatures," Jon said.

"Where is the village?" said Sydney.

"Iceland," said Soul Snatcher.

"Where my parents are!" said Dana.

"And exactly where Loki intends to fight Odin," I said.

"It is only the beginning," said Doom Rider.

"Loki's war threatens to overwhelm us with monsters from below. All three worlds shall suffer. The Underworlds. The homes of the gods. And the world in between — your world. Be ready!"

With that, Doom Rider, Soul Snatcher, and Death Maiden reared their massive horses and rode back into the sky, hauling the net of snarling Draugs between them.

Speechless — and frightened to our bones — we turned back to the two Cyclopes.

And as our only allies disappeared into the night sky, we began our final march to school.

CHAPTER NINE

Into (and Under) the School

We took the back streets, keeping away from any signs of activity, though there wasn't much. Only work crews busily repairing the power lines.

"You Cyclopes really did a good job of shutting everything down," said Jon.

The giants grumbled angrily.

"We need to hurry," I said. "There's no telling when the power might come back." I kept thinking we needed a plan to get the giants back through the school to Hades, but so far we'd been making everything up as we went along.

When we rounded the last corner and saw the school building—and the full parking lot—I turned to Dana. Her face was tight with pain. "Does it hurt all the time?"

Dana nodded, but that was all. She was tough. "Sydney, do you have the rune command worked out yet, to get the Cyclopes down to size?"

Syd breathed out a long puff of air. "I think I do. But we have to speak the names of the runes in the right order or it won't work."

"Put this back on!" I yelled to the hairy giant, holding up the rune. Under the threat of Dana's glove, he looped it around his neck.

Sydney stood squarely in front of both Cyclopes. She swallowed once and said, "Thurisaz . . . Gebo . . . Laguz . . . Sowilo . . . Wunjo . . . Ingwaz . . . I think?"

She thought right. The Cyclopes instantly shrank to the size of little kids, just right for getting into the Greek Underworld.

"You couldn't have figured that out earlier?" Jon asked Sydney.

She grinned. "Perfection takes time. Now, what are we waiting for?"

We entered the school from a side door without anyone seeing us. The emergency lights were beginning to dim. Good. We moved quietly. We were careful and quick, tiptoeing from hall to hall toward the stairs to the basement boiler room—and the entrance to Hades' realm.

We almost made it, too.

Then, just outside the crowded gym, at the worst possible place and the worst possible time, the worst thing happened.

The lights flashed on.

Spooked by the sudden light and sound, the Cyclopes roared and broke the bonds that held them. Shouting the runes' words, they started to grow, knocking Sydney away with a single push. Her cell went flying through the open gym doors.

"No, you don't!" cried Dana, swinging her gloved hand around. Too late. The hairy giant snatched

Dana off her feet. Jon lunged at his huge knees, but the other Cyclops swung around and scooped Jon off the floor. Baldy lurched into the gym with Jon in his hand.

Not surprisingly, everyone shrieked and started running in panic.

"Owen!" My little sister, Mags, ran toward me.

This was bad.

"Sydney!" I shouted. "The runes—"

She barreled through the crowd in the gym, pushing aside our classmates to get to her phone, yelling even before she got to it. "Thurisaz . . . Gebo . . . Sowilo . . . no . . . Ingwaz . . . Laguz . . . no . . . ahhh! Gebo! No. Thuri—I need my phone!"

I rushed the bald giant and caught him off balance. He threw me off, then rose to his full, ugly height. Everyone was freaking out, screaming and running. A blade of light sliced across the air from Dana's glove as she struggled to escape from the hairy giant's hand. The light blasted the podium to bits. The principal dived for cover.

Blam! Another blast.

"Dana, not here!" I cried. It was chaos. I had to do whatever I could. I pulled out the lyre and got ready to strum the strings. "Sydney! Use the runes to get them back to pint-size. Hurry!"

Sydney finally found her cell under our math teacher's foot. She spoke the runic codes on the screen, and the Cyclopes bellowed at the top of their lungs, shaking the light fixtures—but they shrank. Landing on the floor, Dana used her glove to wind the two giants in chains again.

"Downstairs—now!" I hollered.

As Sydney, Jon, and Dana hustled the giants away, everyone in the gym stared at me. It was dead silent.

"Just fooling around," I said, backing out slowly until someone tapped me on the shoulder. I turned, and my heart leaped into my throat.

"Mom, Dad," I said. They looked at me as if they didn't know who I was.

Mags popped her head between them. "Owen, what's going on? What's happening?" My little sister's voice was full of fear. Her eyes were wet. Mom's and Dad's were, too.

I wanted to tell them everything. But there wasn't time. I held up the lyre and plucked two strings slowly. Mags burst out with a laugh. My parents smiled. Everyone in the room began chatting as if nothing was wrong. As if there were no monsters in their school. As if Loki was just a mythological being. As if it was all just a game.

"Good kids!" the crowd cheered. "You go and play!"

My dad patted my shoulder. "See you at home, Owen," he said.

"You, too," I said, giving him a hug. I hoped I would see my family at home, but there was so much to do first. Home seemed so far away. I left the gym and ran downstairs.

Jon, Sydney, and Dana were waiting outside the boiler room door. They leaned against the wall, exhausted, while the Cyclopes stood bound together and scowling.

"There's only one thing left to do," Jon said. "And it better be the last thing, because I'm ready to collapse. Owen, play that lyre, and let's bring these small giant dudes back to the Underworld!"

My fingers twitched nervously, but I finally hit the right strings — second, fourth, first, fourth. I plucked them gently, and as my head went dizzy once more, the sound flowed over us, over the miniature giants, and over the door in front of us until it swung open.

We saw red flames and the darkness of Hades' Underworld beyond.

"Cyclopes, face your destiny!" Jon said. "March!"

Reversing the order of strings — fourth, first, fourth, second — I played the lyre again, and the door closed behind us.

"Let's go," Dana said, pointing to the River Styx up ahead.

Once there, we saw the grouchy old ferryman Charon standing near the riverbank. His floppy hat was pulled low, and his mouth was twisted in anger. I dug one of the pennies from my pocket and dropped it into his upturned palm. He grunted noisily.

"What's wrong?" Sydney said. "We did what Hades asked. We have the Cyclopes. A couple of days early, too."

"What's *wrong?*" growled Charon as we stepped

aboard his raft and he pushed off. "Just the end of the world, that's all. Why do you think I'm working this late? I'll be working day and night for years, now that a war's brewing. Pah! Let the big red guy tell you."

And there he was, pacing on the black shore when we pulled in, the big red guy.

Hades.

Hades took one look at the runes around the giants' necks and snarled. "Loki's servants! So! My Underworld wasn't good enough for you?" He yanked the runes away amid a shower of sparks, threw them to the ground, and crushed them under his heel. As the Cyclopes grew back to their normal height, Hades called out to a large troop of Myrmidon warriors. "Take them away. Far out of my sight!"

The black-armored Myrmidons forced the two sulking giants away at spear point. Soon they were lost in the darkness.

Hades turned back to us, his face grimmer than I had ever seen it.

"So. You've completed your task. Well done," he said joylessly.

"Is Dana allowed to go now?" I asked. "Is she free?"

Hades breathed in and glared down at us. When he saw Dana's glove, his eyes burned white. "That glove may help you. You had better hope it does. Loki will want it back."

I had a feeling that was true. I remembered again about paying the price for magic.

"Dana Runson," Hades went on, "you are free to return to your home. Not that it — or you — will be safe from Loki's war. To assault Asgard itself and topple Odin from his throne, Loki must wage his war in the world above . . . your world. Your home is Loki's battlefield."

We could see vast armies marching toward the northern horizons. Torches streamed in long wavering lines into the far distance. I felt as if my breath had been sucked out of me.

"So it's really happening?" I said.

Hades nodded somberly. "As we speak, our villages nearest the Norse Underworld are burning to the ground. The children of Loki — the fire dragons of Niflheim—are loose. Parts of my empire are already nothing but ashes." Hades paused to gaze at the red glow on the northern horizon. "Loki has always wanted Odin's throne for himself. Now that Underworld monsters have joined his army, war is upon us all. Perhaps now the lyre of Orpheus will prove its deepest worth. Go, all of you. Prepare yourselves!"

With that, Hades dropped a great red helmet over his head, held up a sword that must have been fifteen feet long, and walked away.

We watched silently for a few minutes. More and more of Hades' forces gathered, and the whole ground began to swim with the movement of armies. The Myrmidons. Armored horses, beasts with wings, beasts with horns. Bands of ancient heroes. Hercules. Jason. Odysseus. Achilles. Aeneas. We saw them all.

Your home is Loki's battlefield.

Over and over, those words echoed in my head as we watched the unimaginable. My heart was thundering like a crazy drum as we turned and made our way to the riverbank. All the while, my brain was

still trying to calm itself down, trying to find at least a shred of something to make me feel good about our victory today. My ears throbbed with the sound of marching feet.

"At least you're back with us now," Jon said to Dana as we reached Charon's raft.

"Hades may have let me go, but Loki will be back," said Dana, staring back at the red horizon. "For me, for my parents, and for this glove."

"But you're not leaving us," Sydney added fiercely. "We're sticking together."

I was about to add something when Dana grasped

her wrist, stared into her silver palm, and held her breath.

"What's wrong?" I asked.

"He's . . . he's . . . here!" she whispered. She pointed up the riverbank not far from where we stood, and we heard the sound of something sliding over the black ground beyond.

"I don't like that sound," said Jon. "We should get on Charon's raft right now. We have to go. It's really late—"

I heard the lapping of the River Styx on the shore behind us, and I knew Jon was right. But I couldn't help it. I crept carefully to the top of the riverbank. Sydney and Dana joined me.

Finally, with a soft sigh, Jon followed.

Together we peeked over the top of the slope.

Just as I thought the roller coaster of our day was ending and we were home free, we saw him.

The Dark Master.

CHAPTER TEN

LAND OF THE
TWIN RIVERS

LOKI.

My heart battered the inside of my chest as if it wanted to jump out and walk around.

Jon sighed. "We had to look, didn't we? We couldn't just go home, we had to look."

"The glove told me he was nearby," Dana whispered. "It knew somehow. It must have the same runic charm that makes his armor so powerful. If it knows when Loki is nearby, we can use it. . . ."

Loki stood on the black earth next to his sledge, watching the trail of flaming torches recede into the north. His silver armor reflected their red glow. "Look, Fenrir," he said. "Hades and his heroes march to the fringes of their realm. How quaint. I won't be there when they come. My trick has worked. All they'll meet are an army of dragons. A rather large army."

"Trick?" Sydney whispered. "Hades is heading into an ambush?"

I didn't want it to be true. Loki had played a trick, sending his forces to fake an attack on Hades' northern lands, while he escaped to continue his quest.

A moment later, an army of Draugs marched up behind the sledge. They raised their swords high, then stood at attention.

"These guys are everywhere you look," said Jon under his breath. "Just how many dead Vikings are there?"

"Millions," said Dana.

"The children destroyed the forge? I will find another," Loki said to the Draugs. "They captured the two Cyclopes? I will unleash an army of giants. They stole my glove? I sense it near. And I will have it back."

Dana trembled beside me and looked down at her hand. "Uh-oh. Maybe this isn't such a good thing. . . ."

We crouched perfectly still behind a stack of fallen trees and watched as Loki slipped a dagger out of his cloak and etched a new symbol on the side of the sledge.

"Hades plans to stop us in the north," Loki continued, choking with laughter, "but alas, Fenrir, we travel . . . east. To the land of the twin rivers. The palace of beasts. The horned, the clawed, the fanged. All of them will join me."

My mind was a whirlwind. I had no idea what I was seeing and hearing. But the bottom line was that Loki needed to be stopped. He needed to be stopped from whatever horror he was planning. Turn our whole world into a burning, freezing, dead place, all because he was mad at Odin? No. I couldn't *not* try to stop it. The idea of a war between the gods was too horrifying.

But I was learning that horrifying was also the new normal.

"What are we going to do?" Sydney whispered.

"We have to tell Hades," Jon put in, glancing back at the last of the torches.

"There's no time," I said.

"But we won today," said Sydney. "The hourglass isn't ticking anymore. Dana's free."

"So is Loki," I whispered. "Free to do what he wants. We'll lose him if we—"

"Don't even go there," said Jon. "Come on. Charon's waiting for us. School. Home."

Loki finished carving the rune into the sledge. His armor flashed as if a surge of power raced through it. Dana winced. I turned to her.

"Does it hurt badly?" I whispered.

She took a deep breath and nodded. "I can take it. Are you okay with the lyre?"

I didn't know how to answer. Then I nodded. "Fine."

Loki uttered a dark command to the Draugs.

The dead Vikings bowed and assembled behind the sledge.

"We can't stop him," Sydney whispered. "Not here. Not with all of these Draugs nearby. There must be a thousand of them. What could we possibly do?"

My brain knew she was right. *Turn now*, it said. *Go to the river, take Charon's ferry home, go to sleep. Worry about the war in the morning.*

But something else in me said, *You can't let Loki go! You saw the oracle's vision. He'll destroy our world. Our families, Dana's parents, everyone is in danger!*

All that was true, too. My blood thundered in my ears. My heart battered my ribs. My brain came up with logical arguments for saving myself and forgetting Loki until tomorrow.

Unfortunately, my brain lost.

When Loki's head was turned, and the Draugs had set their sights on the distant hills, I touched Dana's good hand lightly, glanced at Jon and Sydney with what must have been a pretty dumb expression, and crept silently over to Loki's magical sledge.

Without a thought in my head, I lifted the heavy furs on the back end of the sledge and crawled underneath them. I made myself as small as I possibly could and hoped it wasn't the stupidest thing I'd ever done.

When the heavy furs lifted a few moments later, I almost choked.

But it wasn't Loki.

Dana, Jon, and Sydney crawled under the furs next to me.

I was so glad my friends were just as stupid as I was.

I breathed out a long silent breath of relief, held the smelly furs tight with all my strength, and felt Loki's sudden weight on the sledge. We heard the Draugs march away. We heard Loki whip the reins. We heard Fenrir's triumphant roar, and felt the heat of his fiery breath.

Then the magic sledge jerked forward, bounding over the scorched earth. We traveled mile after mile, hour after hour. The surface of the ground changed. There was what felt like snow, then ice. The whole time, none of us spoke. We barely breathed.

Finally, the sledge began to slow.

The *shush* of the sledge's rails up and down a series of gentle slopes lasted for a little while, then it stopped.

Silence.

We heard Loki whisper a command to Fenrir, followed by the jostle of reins. Then both of them left. After five minutes passed, ten, twenty, and we were sure Loki and his wolf were really gone, we lifted the furs and slid to the ground.

To the sand.

The air was hot under a starry night sky. A crescent moon shone over endless seas of sand.

A desert.

Not far away from us stood a desert city. It was monstrous—walled in amber stone, with statues of tall lion-headed creatures. There was a massive blue gate glistening in the moonlight, with studded doors as tall as a house. Crimson towers rose inside the walls. So did a huge cone-shaped temple of white and blue stones, hanging with luxurious gardens.

"So where are we?" Jon asked. "Dana?"

She frowned. "I know Norse and Greek the best," she said. "But if I had to guess, I'd say we're in the Babylonian Underworld."

In the distance, something moved. Lots of somethings.

What at first had seemed like statues of men with lion heads along the amber walls, we saw now were sentinels — living creatures that patrolled the city.

Hundreds of them.

As far as the eye could see.

I drew in a long breath. "In other words, we're a long way from home."

GLOSSARY

Asgard (Norse Mythology): home of the Norse gods and the court of Odin

Charon (Greek Mythology): a ferryman who leads the souls of the dead across the River Styx to the Underworld

Cyclopes (Greek Mythology): one-eyed giants

Draugs (Norse Mythology): death walkers; souls living in dead bodies

Fenrir (Norse Mythology): a giant, fire-breathing red wolf

Hades (Greek Mythology): the ruler of the Underworld

Jason (Greek Mythology): a human hero of many adventures; sailed a ship named the *Argo*

Loki (Norse Mythology): a trickster god

Lyre of Orpheus (Greek Mythology): a stringed instrument that charms people, animals, and objects into doing things for Orpheus

Myrmidons (Greek Mythology): skilled warriors

Odin (Norse Mythology): the chief Norse god

Orpheus (Greek Mythology): a musician who traveled to the Underworld to bring his wife back from the dead

River Styx (Greek Mythology): a river that divides the land of the living from the land of the dead

Valkyries (Norse Mythology): women who work for Odin and choose who lives and dies in battle

DON'T MISS A MINUTE OF THE NEXT ADVENTURE!

TURN THE PAGE FOR

A SNEAK PEEK. . . .

"Prepare yourselves," Panu whispered.

Kingu was an insect over ten feet tall.

His body was formed of overlapping black plates that shifted as he moved. His legs — eight of them — looked like jackhammers, hinged with massive talons on the ends. He had industrial-size pincers for arms. His head was enormous, all knobby and angled, and his fanged mouth looked like a mechanical claw.

Finally, each large eye was yellow and deep, like fire blazing at the end of a tunnel.

Jon gasped. "He's a . . . bug!"

"Scorpion," said Panu. "Marduk cursed him into the shape of a giant, deadly desert scorpion. Kingu is now the Scorpion King."